Read & Resp[ond] 1

FOR KS1

SECTION 1

Funnybones
Teachers' notes 3

SECTION 2

Guided reading
Teachers' notes 4

SECTION 3

Shared reading
Teachers' notes 7
Photocopiable extracts 8

SECTION 4

Plot, character and setting
Activity notes 11
Photocopiable activities 15

SECTION 5

Talk about it
Activity notes 19
Photocopiable activities 22

SECTION 6

Get writing
Activity notes 25
Photocopiable activities 28

SECTION 7

Assessment
Teachers' notes and activity 31
Photocopiable activity 32

Read & Respond

FOR
KS1

Author: Sara Stanley

Development Editor: Alex Albrighton

Editor: Roanne Charles

Assistant Editors: Pam Kelt and Marion Archer

Series Designer: Anna Oliwa

Designer: Liz Gilbert

Illustrations: Janet Ahlberg and
Ellen Hopkins/Beehive Illustration

Text © 2010 Sara Stanley © 2010 Scholastic Ltd

Designed using Adobe InDesign

Published by Scholastic Ltd.
Book End, Range Road,
Witney, Oxfordshire OX29 0YD
www.scholastic.co.uk

Printed by Bell & Bain

1 2 3 4 5 6 7 8 9   0 1 2 3 4 5 6 7 8 9

British Library Cataloguing-in-Publication Data
A catalogue record for this book is available from
the British Library.

ISBN 978-1407-11447-7

Acknowledgements
The publishers gratefully acknowledge permission to reproduce the following copyright material: **Penguin Group UK** for the use of extracts from *Funnybones* by Janet and Allan Ahlberg © 1980, Janet and Allan Ahlberg (1999, Puffin).
Every effort has been made to trace copyright holders for the works reproduced in this book, and the publishers apologise for any inadvertent omissions.

Funnybones

About the book

Funnybones is the first in a series of humorous picture books about a family of (human) skeletons and their skeleton dog. It was first published by Puffin in 1980. It is regarded as a modern classic.

The big skeleton, the little skeleton and their dog skeleton live in the dark dark cellar of a dark dark house on a dark dark hill in a dark dark town, and are out in search of excitement! But the whole town is fast asleep – there is no one to frighten. The family does have some fun and games, including a muddle in reconstructing their dog from a pile of bones.

The only scaring to be had is at the zoo where the skeleton animals are awake. The skeleton family rounds off their outing by frightening each other all the way back home to their dark dark cellar.

The bold illustrations and comic-book style help to make the book very accessible, and the patterned language lends itself to exploration of rhythm in words, music, song and poetry. The book also provides numerous cross-curricular opportunities to develop learning about the human body, animals and locations.

Essential to the humour of the story is the celebration of family fun as the skeletons seek entertainment in the way they know best: frightening somebody!

When the skeleton dog meets with disaster and ends up as a little pile of bones, children will delight in the various attempts to reassemble him, and from this, opportunities abound for learning about skeletal structures and how our bodies work.

The exploits of the big skeleton and the little skeletons will also spark creativity in art and design, problem solving, drama, philosophical thinking and dialogue.

This delightful and unusual story should whet children's appetites and encourage them to explore other Ahlberg titles, particularly the *Funnybones* series, which comprises: *Mystery Tour, Dinosaur Dreams, The Pet Shop, The Black Cat, Skeleton Crew, The Ghost Train, Give the Dog a Bone* and *Bumps in the Night.*

The stories have been adapted as a television series, and *Funnybones* was first aired in 1992, by S4C in Wales and the BBC in England.

About the authors

Husband and wife Janet and Allan Ahlberg worked together on many books; Allan writing and Janet illustrating until Janet's untimely death in 1994. They were a perfect partnership, combining words and pictures on more than 37 collaborations. However, some of the titles in the *Funnybones* series were illustrated by Andre Amstutz.

Allan has written more than 100 books in total. Despite coming from a tough background where he had only one book a year (for attendance at Sunday school), he always dreamed of becoming a writer. He had many jobs before he fulfilled that ambition, including postman, plumber's mate, teacher and gravedigger.

He now lives in London and writes from a small shed at the bottom of the garden.

> **Facts and figures**
> In 2007, the Book Trust gave 700,000 copies of *Funnybones* to Reception children in the UK.
> Allan and Janet Ahlberg also created the popular picture books *Each Peach Pear Plum* and *The Jolly Christmas Postman,* both winners of the Kate Greenaway Medal.

Guided reading

Cover and title pages

Look carefully at the cover, using the terminology *author*, *illustrator*, *cover* and *title*. What can the children tell you about the writing on the cover? Elicit that the authors' names and the title look different – they are in different fonts. Why is the font used for the title so appropriate? Can the children think of a good name for this font?

Encourage the children to explain any other differences between the types of text. Have they noticed that one uses capitals and lower-case letters, and the other all capitals?

Now examine the illustration. Do the children think this is a book about scary skeletons? If not, how does the cover tell us this is not the case? Ask the children whether the picture gives us any clues to what happens in the story and when (night time). What do they think is the relationship between the skeletons?

Look closely at the three illustrations on the title and pre-title pages. Point out that these pictures suggest the fun-loving nature of the skeletons and hint at what they get up to in the story.

Use the title page picture to discuss verbs. What actions are the skeletons performing? Ask the children to help you to write a list of these descriptive words, such as *waving*, *bending*, *sitting*. Point out that these words all end in 'ing'. You may wish more confident children to write this trigraph at the end of each verb.

Spread 1

Read the opening to the children in a straight voice. Does it sound like a scary story? Can the children suggest how to make a reading sound more atmospheric? Re-read the text together, using their ideas to make it sound chilling.

Now focus on the illustrations. Prepare four labels: *town*, *house*, *stairs* and *cellar*. Ask the children to look at these words and match them to the four illustrations on the facing page. Help them to identify initial sounds or clusters and to see the digraphs in each word to help them label the pictures.

Spread 2

Tell the children not to turn the page yet. Re-read the last sentence of spread 1 and the first sentence of this spread in your scariest voice and with a build-up of pace. See if you can make the children jump!

Now ask the children to turn the page and look at the illustration. Does it match the image in their heads that the text created? If not, why not?

Read the text together. Point out the different spellings of the same sound in *scratched*, *skull* and *skeleton*. Ask two children to read the speech bubble text.

Spread 3

Read the first page of text together. Can the children comment on the layout of text? Which words might they move in order to make it look even more like a staircase? (*So the*.)

Before reading the facing page text, ask the children to describe what is happening in the pictures. What is the overall impression created by the blankness of the buildings? (They do not indicate what sort of places they are.)

Spread 4

Notice that this is the first time an illustration has continued across the spread, and it suddenly brings the story to life.

Read the text together. Then cover the text and challenge the children to recall what the skeletons did, in the right order.

Re-read the last four lines of spread 2 and lines 3 to 7 of this spread. Explain the meaning of a catchphrase and challenge the children to say each skeleton's catchphrase (*and frighten somebody!* and *Good idea!*).

Spread 5

Look at the two illustrations. How has the illustrator linked the two pictures together?

Read the first page of text. Then point out the

Guided reading

three consonant blends 'sk', 'st' and 'sw'. Invite the children to play with mixing up the words with the sounds to make new words, such as *sweleton*, *skick*, *stings*. How many muddled words can they make?

Read the second page of text. What has happened to the pace of the story? Can the children pick out any techniques, words or phrases that have moved the story on? (For example, *Suddenly* and the short clauses with action verbs.) Point out the cliffhanger and ask what might happen next.

Can the children recall another example where the reader was left in suspense?

Spread 6

Read the first line together and see if the children predicted the outcome correctly.

Read the rest of the text. Point out the use of speech marks and compare these with the speech bubbles on the opposite page. What purpose do both serve? Ask children to re-read the words in speech bubbles or speech marks using the skeletons' voices, and sing the song together.

Spread 7

Read the first page. Ask the children to point to the question marks. What happens to a reader's voice when they see a question mark?

Look at the four illustrations in turn. Ask the children to point to each picture from top left to bottom right as you read the speech bubbles together. Can the children rearrange *woof* into any other combinations? (*Oofw, owfo, fowo.*)

Now read the facing page. Ask the children to explain why the dog is saying *foow* (*woof* backwards). How would the children describe the two skeletons on this page – puzzled, worried?

Spread 8

Read the text and sing the song. Point out how the speech bubble shows that the skeletons are singing in unison.

Ask the children to sing the song again, emphasising the rhyming words. Which digraph

('ar') and final sound ('k') make these words rhyme? Notice the recurrence of the skeletons' catchphrases.

Read the right-hand page text including the speech bubbles. Observe how the story has returned to the skeletons' quest to find someone to scare. Notice how the illustration resembles early pages and how the text returns to the forbidding repetition of *dark dark…*

Spread 9

Before reading the text, ask the children to describe 'who, where, what' in the pictures on the left-hand page.

After reading the text, enjoy working out what the skeleton animals are. Discuss how the use of colour works to create an X-ray effect, both in the illustrations and the main text.

Spread 10

After reading, ask the children why the skeletons say '*Let's have a word with the parrot skeleton.*' Help the children to understand the play on words. Ask a good reader to read the speech bubble in a 'parrot' voice.

Ask them if they can think of a card game to play with the crocodile. How about 'Snap'! Generate further examples of this sort of animal word play, such as *Let's pack our trunk with the elephant. Let's go nuts with the monkeys. Let's tell a tall story to the giraffe. Let's not play games with the cheetah. Let's see if we can spot a leopard.*

Spread 11

Ask the children to tell you the first thing they notice about this page. Why do they think that the skeletons are so dominant and their speech bubbles so prominent? (It emphasises that the story is now focused on the skeletons frightening *each other*.)

In addition to what the skeletons plan to do, what significant information does the text reveal? It gives us the reason *why* they have made the choice to frighten each other.

Spread 12

What do the children first notice about this spread? (Probably the large speech bubbles.) Ask individual children to read the speech, then discuss how the size, full capitals and exclamation marks emphasise the loud and scary surprise of the sounds.

Read the text, then ask whether it gives the reader extra information, or if the pictures could stand alone. Discuss how each picture tells a mini-story and ask the children to describe what is happening. What dramatic effects show that the dog did the best job of frightening? (In addition to the size of *WOOF!*, the skeletons have jumped together and the big skeleton's hat has shot off.)

Ask the children to tell you which word is used most in this text? (*Skeleton.*) What effect does the repetition of the skeleton words have on the story? (It alters the pace making it seem fast and chaotic, rather like a chase itself!)

Spread 13

Encourage the children to think of a sentence to describe the large illustration on the left-hand page. Then read the text together. Point out the verbs (one on each line).

Ask the children to look at the illustrations and suggest their own verbs, or provide ideas such as *snatched*, *ran* and *yelped*.

Challenge the children to find an example of a phoneme that is spelled differently – for example, the 'i' sound in *climbed* and in *frightened*. Ask them to read the word *other*. Which word contains the same sound but is also spelled differently? (*Dustbin.*)

Spread 14 and final page

Read the first line together then hide the text on the right-hand page. Invite the children to tell the story sentence by sentence, using the pictures as clues.

Provide each child with five labels: *hill*, *town*, *street*, *house*, *staircase* and *cellar*. Help the children to decode their set of words and match them to the illustrations.

Turn the page and read the last sentence together. Ask why this sentence is on its own page. Does it generate suspense? Might it make you think that the skeletons could be waiting for you?!

Finally, ask the children to close the book and try to repeat the last refrain from memory, starting with *and that is how the story ends*. Invite them to work out how many times they think the word *dark* was used in this text. (22 times.)

Shared reading

Extract 1

● Read the first line and ask the children what they notice. How do we know this is not the beginning of a sentence? (The first letter of the first word is in lower case.) Ask the children if this part of the sentence makes sense on its own. Explain that it is a conjunctive word that joins two parts of a sentence. See if the children can suggest ways to begin the sentence.

● Read the next five lines. Ask a volunteer to underline and read out any dialogue. Discuss how dialogue is identified, and highlight the use of speech marks. Now ask individual children to use different-coloured pens to distinguish the big skeleton's speech from the little skeleton's.

● Read the rest of the extract, then focus on the phrase *sang a song*. What do the children notice about the words? Highlight the shared initial 's' sound and final digraph 'ng'. Explain that 'a' and 'o' are vowels. Ask the children to help you write all the vowels on the board, then ask which vowel can not be inserted in *sang* to make a new word ('e'). You might like to read 'On the Ning Nang Nong' by Spike Milligan for word play around a similar construction.

Extract 2

● Read the first sentence, and recall from Extract 1 what the skeletons have *finished*.

● Highlight the 'wh' digraph in *When*, then challenge the children to find the other digraphs in the sentence (in *they* and *finished*). Can the children see what these three digraphs have in common? (They all have an 'h' sound.) Elicit another digraph with 'h' in it ('ch').

● Read the next four lines, then draw attention to the dash. Explain that it shows a pause. It indicates that the skeleton has had an 'afterthought'. Re-read the sentence ignoring the dash. What effect does this have? (The lack of pause takes away the surprise, the punchline.)

● Read the rest of the extract and recall that the skeletons also sang a song at the end of Extract 2. Why do the children think the skeletons sing?

● Look at the word *together* and point out that it contains three small words. Ask the children to write the three separate words. Now rejoin them. Note how the 't' and 'h' join to form 'th' and change the pronunciation of the word(s).

Extract 3

● This extract of patterned text contains a number of past tense verbs. After reading the text, ask the children to underline these words (*jumped, frightened, climbed* and *hid*) and look at the endings. Which is the odd word out and why? What would happen if we added 'ed' to *hide*? Can the children suggest other verbs we cannot add 'ed' to (for example, *run, swim, buy, teach,* *find, fly*) and provide their past tense versions?

● Notice again the use of the dash. Elicit that its purpose here is to keep the reader in suspense (over a page break).

● Finally, compare the use of *and* in these sentences with the opening line of Extract 1. Explain that both parts of each sentence are shown here.

Extract 1

and ended up as a little pile of bones.

"Look at that!" the big skeleton said.
"He's all come to pieces.
What shall we do now?"
"Let's put him together again,"
the little skeleton said.
So the big skeleton
and the little skeleton
put the dog skeleton together again.
They sang a song while they did it.

Extract 2

When they had finished, the big
skeleton said,
"That dog looks a bit funny to me."
"So he does," said the little skeleton.
"We've got his tail on the wrong end –
and his head!"
"Foow!" said the dog skeleton.

At last the dog was properly
put back together again.
The big skeleton and the little skeleton
sang another song.

Extract 3

They hid round corners
and frightened each other.
They climbed up lamp posts
and frightened each other.
They jumped out of dustbins
and frightened each other –

all the way home.

And that is how the story ends.

Plot, character and setting

Dem bones – rhythm sticks

Objective: To enjoy listening to and using spoken and written language and readily turn to it in play and learning.
What you need: Copies of *Funnybones*, large sheets of paper and pens and a range of percussion instruments that can be banged, such as claves, drumsticks, castanets, chime bars and xylophones.
Cross-curricular link: Music.

What to do

● Elicit how words are split into syllables – for example, *fun/ny/bones*.
● Ask the children in small groups to look through the book for words that contain three or more syllables – for example, *connected, skeleton, suddenly, together, properly, everybody, animals, policemen, elephant, crocodile*. Record examples on the large paper and ask volunteers to split the words into syllables with strokes (*conn/ect/ed, an/i/mals, ev/er/y/bod/y* and so on).

● Hand out the instruments and help the children to create a bones orchestra. Tap out the rhythm as you chant the syllabic words.
● Look through the book and ask for one example of a word with one, two, three, four and finally five syllables. Record these on the paper and invite one member of the class to choose a word in secret and tap out its rhythm for others to guess what it is. Repeat until all the listed words have been worked out.

Differentiation
For older/more confident learners: Ask the children to find dialogue that they could tap out and chant. Invite them to invent their own rhythmic phrases.
For younger/less confident learners: Start the activity by tapping out children's names, then play 'Big skeleton, little skeleton'. Ask a child to sit in the middle of a circle. When he or she stands the children tap *big*, when the child squats down they tap *litt/le*.

Skeleton dancing

Objective: To explore familiar themes and characters through music, improvisation and role play.
What you need: 'Fossils' (from *Carnival of the Animals*) and 'Danse Macabre' by Camille Saint-Saëns, playback equipment, copies of *Funnybones*, hall space, flipchart and pen.
Cross-curricular link: Dance.

What to do

● Play 'Danse Macabre' and ask the children to describe how the music makes them feel. Encourage them to use words or phrases that capture the spooky atmosphere.
● Now play 'Fossils' and ask the children to look through *Funnybones* as the music plays.
● Compare the two pieces of music. Discuss pace and tone. Which instruments can be identified? Why do they think a xylophone was used? Did the pieces evoke different moods, emotions, pictures? If so, what and why?
● Together, find places in *Funnybones* that could be matched to the music. Prompt the children to think carefully about skeletons' movements. Record descriptive action words such as *jumping, creeping, tiptoeing, chasing* and *rattling*.
● Encourage the children to demonstrate examples of movements that they could match to the music.

Differentiation
For older/more confident learners: Give the children time to put their movements into a sequence and to perform their dance with gesture and facial expression.
For younger/less confident learners: Model a variety of movements and actions for the children to copy.

Plot, character and setting

Mixed-up skeleton zoo

> **Objective:** To explore and experiment with sounds, words and text.
> **What you need:** Copies of photocopiable page 15, pens and a set of alphabet cards 's', 'n', 'o', 'r' and 't'.
> **Cross-curricular link:** Science.

What to do

● Tell the children that the skeleton keeper at the zoo made a shocking discovery – some of the skeleton animals' bones were muddled up in the night, like the skeleton dog. Explain that, although he has managed to put them back together, in the confusion the animals have got their noises all back to front!

● Ask the children to look at the first example on the photocopiable sheet and sound out the new noise. Does it still sound like an animal noise? Bring out the onomatopoeic nature of the real words.

● Allow volunteers to assemble the alphabet cards on the board to read *trons*. Read the word together, thinking about each sound that makes it up.

● Now ask for volunteers to use the cards to reverse the word. Read the word again. What do the children notice about the word now? Point out the digraph 'or' that has been created.

● Ask the children to complete the remaining sound-words on their sheets, working individually or in pairs.

> **Differentiation**
> **For older/more confident learners:** Challenge the children to make many muddled-up combinations of each word. Which word produces the greatest number of combinations?
> **For younger/less confident learners:** Provide a set of alphabet cards for each child or group to help them to rearrange the words.

Beware the skeleton!

> **Objective:** To link sounds to letters, naming and sounding the letters of the alphabet.
> **What you need:** Flipchart or board, note paper, pens and copies of *Funnybones*.
> **Cross-curricular link:** Science.

What to do

● Write the alphabet across the top of the board.

● Play a version of 'Hangman'. Explain to the children that they have to try to prevent a picture of a scary skeleton being completed by guessing the missing letters to a mystery word.

● Let the children search through the book for examples of any action words (verbs). Share these and secretly write one down. Give the folded paper to a trusted child.

● Record in dashes the number of letters of the word and ask the children to count them.

● Ask the children to offer a letter sound that they think may be in the missing word. If the letter is not in the word, dramatically draw part of the skeleton on the board. If the letter is correct, write it in the correct place in the word.

● Encourage the children to look back at their verbs if they get stuck.

● Continue the activity until the children either guess or complete the word (revealed on the paper) or the skeleton is complete and you have shouted *'BOO!'*

> **Differentiation**
> **For older/more confident learners:** Include words with digraphs and record the digraphs alongside the letters of the alphabet.
> **For younger/less confident learners:** Use actions to hint at the missing words.

Plot, character and setting

Journey maps

> **Objective:** To retell stories, ordering events using story language.
> **What you need:** Copies of *Funnybones*, A3 paper and drawing tools.
> **Cross-curricular link:** Geography.

What to do

● Organise the children into groups of four to six. Give each group a copy of the book, a large sheet of paper and pot of drawing equipment.
● Encourage each group to recall the story and think together about all the places the skeletons visited, such as the hill, the street, the zoo and the swings.
● Challenge the groups to work together to draw a map plotting the skeletons' journey around the dark dark town.
● Bring the class back together and ask for words and phrases from the book that describe the journey – for example, *walked past, on, over, climbed, stepped out into, went into, left the…*
● Encourage each group to follow their maps to retell the story, using examples of these words and phrases.
● Can the children think of any other words they could use to describe how the skeletons get from one place to another? (For example, *up, down, through, in front of, under.*)

> **Differentiation**
> **For older/more confident learners:** Give the children a set of positional labels, such as *through, under, over, around* and challenge them to create a new journey for the skeletons – for example, a trip to the beach.
> **For younger/less confident learners:** Work with this group. Ask the children to draw locations and suggest positional language for you to scribe.

What happens next?

> **Objective:** To retell stories, ordering events using story language.
> **What you need:** Copies of *Funnybones*, an enlarged copy of photocopiable page 16 cut into four, copies of photocopiable page 16 for each child and pencils.

What to do

● Choose one of the four text extracts (listed on photocopiable page 16) to read together. Set the children to find the page in the book it comes from. Establish whether it is at the beginning, middle or end of the story. Now ask the children to close their books.
● Repeat this for the other three extracts.
● Now ask the children to choose which extract comes first and talk in pairs about what happens next: *Suddenly something happened… The dog skeleton crashed into the bench.* Write some of their suggestions on the enlarged sheet.
● Repeat for the other three extracts.
● Hand out copies of photocopiable page 16 and ask the children to draw a picture to describe what happens next for each text extract.
● Allow time for the children to share their illustrations and talk about them in pairs or as a whole class.

> **Differentiation**
> **For older/more confident learners:** Good writers could add a brief description of what happens next to caption each illustration.
> **For younger/less confident learners:** Allow the children to look through the book with an adult and discuss what happens and why. Support them in completing the sheet one box at a time.

Plot, character and setting

Who says what?

Objective: To explore the effect of patterns of
language and repeated words and phrases.
What you need: Flipchart or board, copies of
Funnybones, photocopiable page 17, scissors and glue.

What to do

● Read the story, placing emphasis on dialogue.
Point out the use of speech bubbles and clarify
their purpose to show what the characters are
saying in an illustration format. How are they
different from speech marks? (One is written
within the text and the other is in a picture.)
● Can the children tell you which skeleton
usually asks the questions? (The big skeleton.)
Collect questions the big skeleton asks. Then ask
which skeleton usually gives ideas or suggestions.
(The little skeleton.) Collect suggestions the
little skeleton makes. Does what they say tell us
anything about the skeletons' characters?

● Look at all the speech bubbles again and
find other examples of dialogue. Recap on what
a catchphrase is and see if the children can
recognise the catchphrase of each skeleton.
● Ask for a volunteer to offer a line of dialogue
spoken by one of the skeletons. Challenge the
other children to work out which skeleton it is.
● Now encourage the children to complete
photocopiable page 17 by choosing an extract of
dialogue that each skeleton speaks and sticking it
in the correct speech bubble.

Differentiation
For older/more confident learners: Challenge the
children to draw and write a speech bubble for the
dog skeleton.
For younger/less confident learners: Provide support
for children to identify and read the text. Encourage
them to practise the catchphrases in character.

Bony bingo

Objective: To read simple words by sounding out
and blending the phonemes all through the word
from left to right.
What you need: Flipchart or board, copies of
Funnybones, individual copies of photocopiable page
18, coloured pencils, pre-prepared word cards (see
below), a hat/box (to contain the word cards) and
Blu-Tack®.

What to do

● Before the lesson begins, prepare a set of word
cards featuring nouns from the story – *skeleton,
zoo, dog, cellar* and so on. Place these nouns into
a hat or box.
● Begin the lesson by writing the following
words on the board and asking the children to
tell you which word is the odd one out: *dustbin,
parrot, run* and *hat*. (The odd one out is *run*
because it is a verb and the other words are
all nouns.)
● After reading the story, set the children,

working individually, to search through the text
to find as many nouns as they can. Ask volunteers
to read their words aloud and check that everyone
has understood which words are nouns. Create a
class list of words.
● Hand out copies of photocopiable page 18 and
ask the children to select nine nouns and write
them on their bingo card.
● Shake the hat or box before pulling out and
reading the first bony bingo word. Fix it to the
board and tell the children to lightly colour in
the bones if they contain words called out. The
winner is the first person to complete their board
(or to get three words in a row).

Differentiation
For older/more confident learners: Challenge the
children to complete larger bingo grids.
For younger/less confident learners: Mark up boards
with a few simple nouns in place and play in small
groups with adult support.

Mixed-up skeleton zoo

- Read the speech bubbles. What noise is the animal making?
- Rearrange the letters to help the animals get their noises back!

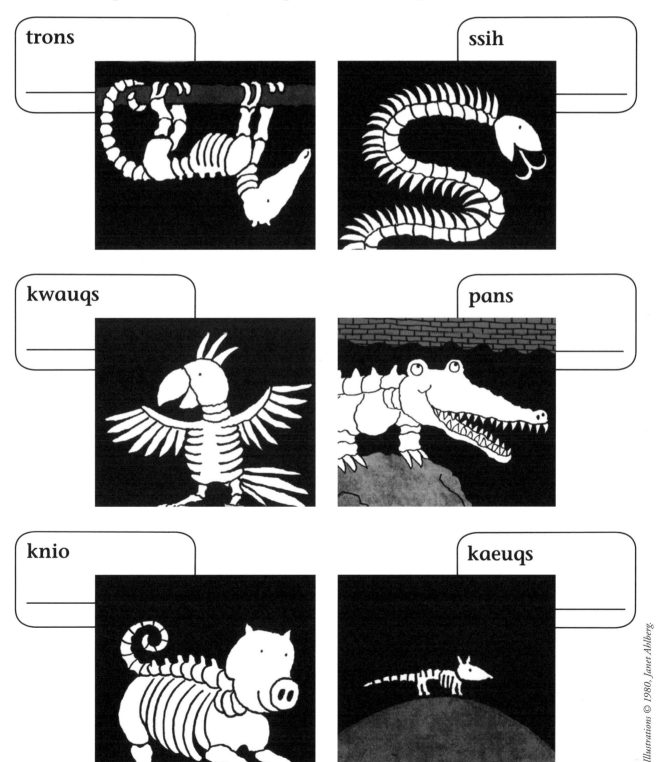

trons
_____

ssih
_____

kwauqs
_____

pans
_____

knio
_____

kaeuqs
_____

Illustrations © 1980, Janet Ahlberg.

What happens next?

● Read the text and draw what happens next.

Suddenly something happened…	
The *skeleton* animals were awake…	
"That dog looks a bit funny to me…"	
They still could not find anybody to frighten…	

Plot, character and setting

Who says what?

● Cut out the word boxes and stick them in the correct skeleton's speech bubble.

What shall we do?	Good idea!
Let's frighten somebody!	Let's frighten each other!

Illustration © 1980, Janet Ahlberg.

SECTION
4

Bony bingo

Write nine nouns on the bones. Colour them in when you hear one called.

Talk about it

Who am I?

> **Objective:** To ask and answer questions, make relevant contributions, offer suggestions and take turns.
> **What you need:** Flipchart or board, sticky notes and/or small pieces of paper and pencils.

What to do

● Write the heading *Zoo* on the board and ask the children to help you to populate the zoo with as many different animals as they can think of, starting off with those in *Funnybones*. List ideas on the board.

● Then say that you are thinking of one animal from the zoo. Challenge the children to work out which it is by asking questions. First, discuss which sort of questions are useful for finding out about an animal: identification of habitat, food, habits, appearance (including size, colour, distinguishing features) and sound. Explain to the children that they will be able to ask only one question each, to which you will say only *Yes* or *No*, and they cannot say what they think the animal is until everyone has asked a question. Instead, give each child a small piece of paper to write or draw the animal on when they think they know it. Remind them not to call out, but to listen carefully.

● Model the first question– for example, *Does the animal make a loud noise?* Remind the children they may only ask for information with a yes/no answer and they must not name the animal.

● When each child has asked a question, check the children's answers.

> **Differentiation**
> **For older/more confident learners:** Give each child a sticky note, on which is written the name of an animal. Ask them to place their note on someone's back. Let the children move around asking questions until they work out which animal they are.
> **For younger/less confident learners:** Draw pictures on the board to illustrate the children's ideas.

Scary concept line

> **Objective:** To listen to each other's views and preferences; consider alternatives and reach agreement.
> **What you need:** Photocopiable page 22 (enlarged and cut up) and a length of string.
> **Cross-curricular links:** PSHE, philosophy.

What to do

● Present the pictures from photocopiable page 22 and establish what they show.

● Stretch the string on the floor with the labels *Scary* and *Not scary* at either end. Explain that the children need to place each figure somewhere on the string (concept line) according to its perceived scariness.

● Ask for volunteers to place cards one at a time along the line. Encourage some discussion about where things are placed. Is there any disagreement? Why?

● Allow others to change the order of cards, giving reasons. Stress that cards can only be moved if an explanation can be justified and the majority agrees.

● Ask: *Why do we get scared? What makes something scary? How do you know when you are scared? Can something that is not real be scarier than something that is? Is it always bad to be scared?* (Think about the fun in *Funnybones*.)

> **Differentiation**
> **For older/more confident learners:** Ask the children to draw and write about when they have felt scared.
> **For younger/less confident learners:** Encourage the children to draw and describe something scary.

Talk about it

Agree or disagree

> **Objective:** To make a decision and give valid reason for their choices; to challenge, support and move ideas forward.
> **What you need:** Copies of photocopiable page 23.
> **Cross-curricular link:** PSHE.

What to do

● Ask the children to write their names in the spaces provided on photocopiable page 23. Tell them to cut out the two panels 'I agree' and 'I disagree'. Then establish what the words *agree* and *disagree* mean.

● Elicit that the main focus of the story is the visit to the zoo. Do the children think the skeletons enjoy going to the zoo?

● Write and read the following statement to the children: *Animals belong in a zoo.* Allow a moment's silent thinking time. Then ask the children to place the appropriate paper in front of them showing whether they agree or disagree. Record the numbers.

● Ask a volunteer to explain how they made their choice. Encourage others to participate, saying why they agreed or disagreed.

● Where appropriate, ask questions such as: *Are animals happy in zoos? What about if they have never been in the wild? Do we have a duty to care for animals? Should we keep pets in zoos? Why do we keep some animals in zoos but not others? Could we put people in zoos?* Encourage confident children to make notes on their voting paper during the talk.

● After the discussion, hold another vote. Has anybody changed their mind? If so, can they explain why?

> **Differentiation**
> **For older/more confident learners:** Encourage the children to ask and record questions about zoos.
> **For younger/less confident learners:** Practise with fun agree/disagree statements first, such as *Bananas are purple, Elephants should come to school.*

What is a person?

> **Objective:** To ask and answer questions, make relevant contributions, offer suggestions and take turns.
> **What you need:** Large sheet of paper and a pen.
> **Cross-curricular links:** PSHE, philosophy, science.

What to do

● Arrange the children in a circle. Talk about why we see the skeletons in the story as people.

● Draw a child-sized skeleton on the large piece of paper while you sing 'Dem Bones' together.

● Ask the children whether this skeleton is a person.

● Now ask a child to lie on top of the skeleton drawing and choose a volunteer to draw around that child. The skeleton should now have a 'human' outline.

● Ask whether the figure is a person now. Encourage the children to offer suggestions and agree or disagree with statements made.

● Through careful questioning, ask the children to suggest what makes us human. *Do all humans look the same? Does a person have to talk? Can a baby walk and talk? What would the skeleton need to be alive? Do you need a brain to be a person?*

> **Differentiation**
> **For older/more confident learners:** Ask the children to draw a skeleton and a person and write down thoughts about the differences – for example, what makes the Big Skeleton more than just bones?
> **For younger/less confident learners:** Ask the children to draw a skeleton and a person and ask an adult to scribe their statement: *The person is different because...*

Talk about it

Scary story sack

Objective: To speak clearly and audibly with confidence and control and show awareness of the listener.
What you need: A container with some or all of the following: cooked spaghetti (intestines), peeled grapes (eyes), surgical glove part-filled with sand/water (hand), unpopped corn kernels (teeth), dried orange peel (skin), dried apricots (ears), large carrots/parsnips (bones), natural sponge (brain) and a blindfold.

What to do
● Sit in a circle with the children and explain that you are going to play a game that the skeletons enjoy scaring each other with. Reassure the children that it is only a trick!
● Ask for a very willing and confident volunteer to be 'scared'. Blindfold the volunteer and reassure them they will be safe.

● Gingerly or dramatically take out the first item and pass it around the circle, telling the children not to tell the 'victim' what the 'body part' is but to describe in frightening terms how it looks, feels and smells and/or give a clue to its function.
● After a few gory descriptions, pass the object to the victim and ask him or her to guess what part of the body it is. Allow them to remove the blindfold and see the 'scary' object.
● Repeat for other objects.

Differentiation
For older/more confident learners: Challenge the children to write a ghost story using descriptive language.
For younger/less confident learners: Ask an adult to be the first 'victim' so the children are in on the trick.

The dark dark game

Objective: To listen with sustained concentration and retell stories, ordering events using story language.
What you need: Copies of *Funnybones* and a copy of photocopiable page 24, enlarged and cut up.

What to do
● Read the story and look at all the locations. Discuss how the opening and ending develop a sense of something within something else.
● Arrange the children in a circle and place the word cards face down in the centre. Choose one child to pick up a card and start the game by saying: *This is how the story begins. On a dark dark hill there was a dark dark ___* [insert the word on the card].
● Invite the next person to continue the story with: *In the dark dark ___ there was a dark dark ___,* adding their own suggestion of a place within the place. Encourage the children to use appropriate expression to create an eerie atmosphere.
● Ask the next person to repeat the story so far and then add the ending *some skeletons lived!*
● Now ask the next person to start again with a different card, and repeat the story sequence. Continue until everyone has had a turn.
● Discuss which cards worked best for an interesting story. Did the different places change the tone of the story? If so, how?

Differentiation
For older/more confident learners: Encourage the children to make their own lists of unusual locations.
For younger/less confident learners: Draw their suggestions as a storyboard to help the children visualise and analyse the new stories. Add illustrations to the cards to serve as prompts.

Scary concept line

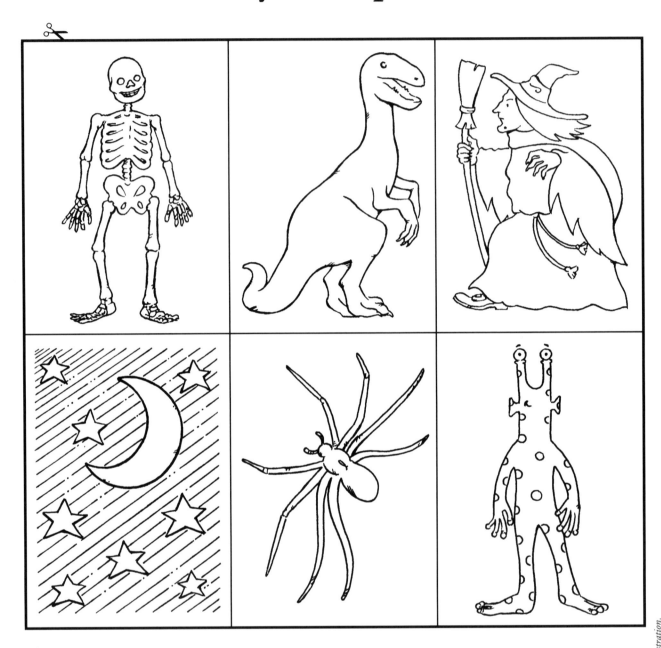

Illustration © 2010, Ellen Hopkins/Beehive Illustration.

Scary	Not scary

SECTION 5

Agree or disagree

● Write your name in the spaces provided below and then cut out each card.

I agree

I disagree

Name _____

_____

Name _____

_____

The dark dark game

castle	hole	matchbox
spaceship	bathroom	hat
pocket	lift	bed
wellington boot	cage	egg

Get writing

Skeleton rhymes

Objective: To make up own songs, rhymes and poems; to compose and write simple sentences showing awareness of rhyme.
What you need: *Each Peach Pear Plum* by Janet and Allan Ahlberg, copies of *Funnybones*, copies of photocopiable page 28, pencils, flipchart or board and percussion instruments (optional).
Cross-curricular link: Music.

What to do

● Read both *Funnybones* and *Each Peach Pear Plum*, pointing out that they are by the same authors. What similarities and differences do the children notice? Look at the illustrations: one has colour and detail, the other is dark and simple. Look at the language: both books contain repeated phrases. Lead the discussion towards asking: *Does Funnybones contain any rhyme?*
● Since it does not, challenge the children to create some rhymes using the extracts from *Funnybones* on photocopiable page 28.
● Start off by inviting the children to suggest rhyming words for the last given word in each phrase or sentence – for example, *Look at that!* – *hat, cat, bat.* Record ideas on the board.
● Ask the children to continue the phrases by adding their own rhyming sentence ending.
● Allow time for sharing examples in pairs, small groups or as a whole class.
● Have fun setting the rhymes to music to create skeleton songs.

Differentiation
For older/more confident learners: Challenge the children to take a section of the book and create rhyming phrases to replace the text.
For younger/less confident learners: Organise groups of seven to create a shared piece of work with each child contributing one rhyming sentence each.

A different tale

Objective: To identify the main events and characters in stories, and write from an alternative point of view.
What you need: Copies of *Funnybones, Voices in the Park* by Anthony Browne (if available), paper and pens and a 'hot-seat' (chair covered with a cloth).

What to do

● After reading *Funnybones*, ask the children to list all of the characters in the story and note their involvement in the plot.
● Now read *Voices in the Park*. Discuss how the author has used different 'voices' to create alternative viewpoints of the same event.
● Read *Funnybones* again and ask the children to consider the story from the point of view of either a policeman's dream, a zoo animal or the dog skeleton.
● Put confident children in the hot-seat to develop an understanding of the characters first.
● Encourage the children to use their imaginations to answer in role questions such as: *What were you doing before the events of the evening? What would you rather have been doing? What did you see or imagine happened? What do you think about what happened? How do you feel about the two skeletons? What are the consequences of the evening's events?*
● Now challenge the children to choose one of the listed characters and write a version of the story from that point of view. Remind them to write in that character's 'voice'.

Differentiation
For older/more confident learners: Challenge the children to write three characters' versions within the same story, in the style of *Voices in the Park*.
For younger/less confident learners: Provide word banks and model sentence starters.

Get writing

How to make a dancing skeleton

Objective: To write instructions to convey information in simple non-narrative form.
What you need: Photocopiable page 29 copied on to card, scissors, split pins, paper and pencils.
Cross-curricular link: Science.

What to do

● Explain to the children that they will be challenged to write a complete set of instructions for a task. Sing 'Dem Bones' to get them in the mood.
● Elicit what purpose instructions serve (they help a reader to do something) and share ideas about where you might find them – for example, in recipe books, games rules and with toys.
● Give pairs of children the skeleton diagram, and challenge them to list the stages needed to build the moving skeleton. Suggest they practise putting it together with one child cutting out the parts and assembling, while the other notes down what is being done.
● When the instructions are written, ask the children to swap theirs with another pair's. Tell the children to follow their new instructions, and allow time for the skeletons to be assembled.
● Bring the children together and show the skeletons. Enjoy making them dance. Ask if there were any assembly difficulties. What happened if instructions were out of sequence or missed out? Were the instructions too complicated or not clear enough?

Differentiation
For older/more confident learners: Providing a reference text, challenge them to write instructions using simple anatomical language and to label the bones.
For younger/less confident learners: Complete the skeleton step by step, asking the children to help you write a class instruction sheet as you go along.

Expanding universe

Objective: To attempt writing for various purposes, using features of different forms.
What you need: Large envelopes, paper and pencils.
Cross-curricular links: Geography, science.

What to do

● Explain that there have been complaints about the skeletons' antics! And now the children need to write a short informal letter to the skeletons, suggesting what they could do instead of scaring people.
● Allow time for small-group discussion, then share ideas for alternative activities.
● Discuss the format and conventions of letter writing, using *Dear* and *Love from*. Then let the children write their short letters.
● Explain that the letter will have to be addressed to the skeletons and the postman will need precise instructions on where to find the cellar.
● Read the text from *On a dark dark hill…* to *some skeletons lived*. Model the address, pointing out capital letters and line placement:
   The Big Skeleton
   The cellar
   The staircase
   The house…
● See who can create the longest address by continuing locations out to the universe.
● Share letters and the longest address(es). Identify locations such as village, city, county, country, continent and planet.

Differentiation
For older/more confident learners: Challenge the children to write a longer letter to the skeletons, giving reasons why scaring people is not a good thing. Ask them to address a letter to themselves using their expanded real address.
For younger/less confident learners: Let the children draw a picture and describe a fun activity for the skeletons, to put in the addressed envelope.

Get writing

Bone dominoes

Objective: To interact with others, negotiating plans.
What you need: A set of cards from photocopiable page 30 for each group.
Cross-curricular link: Science.

What to do

● Start by recalling the jumbled-up dog bones from the story. Then divide the class into teams of six or eight to play 'Bone dominoes'.
● Explain that the race is to be the first team to put together a complete skeleton.
● Give each team a shuffled set of bone cards, roughly spread out face down.
● Tell the children that they must take turns within their team to turn over one card at a time. The next card can only be placed if it directly connects to the previous card. So, a skull cannot connect to a leg bone and so on. In this case, the card is returned to the pile, and play passes to the next person.
● The first team to complete their skeleton will be the winners and may perform a celebratory skeleton dance!
● Ask the children to write instructions explaining how to play the game.

Differentiation
For older/more confident learners: Challenge the children to make a linked set of sentences, *The ___ bone's connected to the ___ bone.*
For younger/less confident learners: Provide a simple labelled skeleton picture for reference.

A Funnybones sequel

Objective: To create short simple texts on paper and screen that combine words with images.
What you need: Copies of *Funnybones*, paper, drawing materials and access to computers.
Cross-curricular links: Art and design, ICT.

What to do

● Examine the cover of the book. Discuss the simple design of text and purpose of the illustration.
● Read the back page and elicit the meaning of *Other titles in the series.* Read the list of titles and ask the children to suggest from the titles alone what might happen in each book.
● Now ask the children to design a typeface that looks like bones. Allow time for them to design the letters they need.
● If they need inspiration, look through a selection of books and compare the alphabets.
● Ask the children to come up with a sequel of their own and design an exciting new cover, using their bone typeface for the title. Then suggest they create an illustration that conveys an idea of the story.
● If possible, before the lesson, create an on-screen frame to replicate a 'blank' *Funnybones* cover. Help the children to scan in and place their titles and cover illustrations.
● Arrange for the designs to be displayed.

Differentiation
For older/more confident learners: Encourage the children to write a brief synopsis of their sequel to go with their cover design.
For younger/less confident learners: Invite the children to tell others what their story will be about.

Get writing

SECTION 6

Skeleton rhymes

- Finish each sentence with a rhyme.

In a dark dark house…   _____
What shall we do now?   _____
That dog looks a bit funny to me…   _____
Even the animals in the zoo…   _____
There was a dark dark town…   _____
Look at that!   _____
"That reminds me," he said…   _____

READ & RESPOND: Activities based on Funnybones

How to make a dancing skeleton

● Cut out the bones, assemble the skeleton and then write instructions explaining how to put this skeleton together.

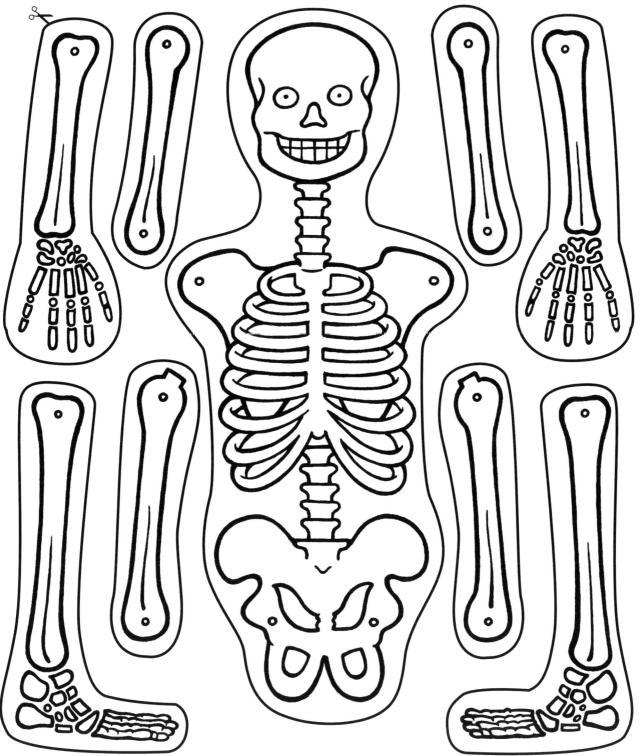

Illustration © 2010, Ellen Hopkins/Beehive Illustration.

Bone dominoes

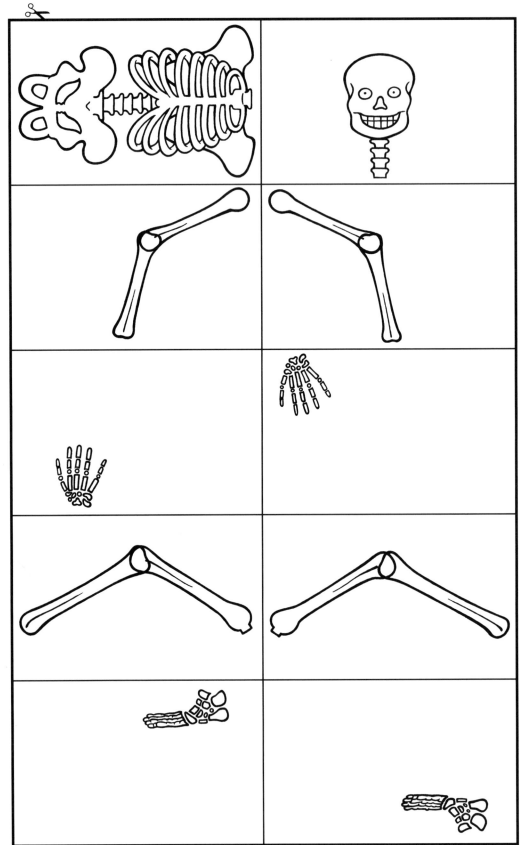

Illustration © 2010, Ellen Hopkins/Beehive Illustration.

Assessment

Assessment advice

This classic picture book provides plentiful opportunities for children to explore the playfulness of succinct text and witty dialogue. The book's humour, fun-filled plot, patterned language and familiar settings allow children to examine the ghost story genre on a child-friendly level. Readers will enjoy the suspense of the cliffhangers and dramatic plot twists. Learning opportunities juxtapose fantastical humour with scientific understanding of the skeletal structures of humans and other animals.

The activities in this book encourage children to scare and be scared, experiment with songs, rhythm and pace, explore dialogue, and reveal their thoughts about fear and the nature of being human.

The activities help children to develop skills as critical readers of text, illustration and humorous word play. The nature of the book allows children to engage with a text that brings characters to life through dialogue and as we know, dialogue leads to more dialogue!

Encouraging children to summarise the plot of the story in a positive way will give you a thorough insight into the children's understanding of not just the plot, but also how the story is made appealing to the reader and plays with repetition and dramatic irony.

Funnybones blurb

> **Assessment focus:** To show an understanding of the main events of story such as main characters, sequence of events, use of repetition and suspense.
> **What you need:** Copies of *Funnybones*, copies of photocopiable page 32 and pencils.

What to do

● Look together at the back cover. What would the children expect to see here? Prompt the children, if necessary, to notice that there is no real blurb.

● Elicit the purpose of a blurb – for example, a tantalising summary of the story which motivates the reader to explore the book. Discuss what information a reader would want to know in order to make a choice about reading the story. Encourage the children to share their ideas about character, setting and plot, including hints about unexpected events.

● Hand out copies of photocopiable page 32.

Read the sentence starters on the assessment sheet and spend time checking that all of the children understand the task. Ask questions such as: *What is an assumption or generalisation? What is a cliffhanger? What can we say about the language and style of this story? What makes it funny? What was particularly enjoyable, interesting or unusual about the book? How important are the illustrations? Why do you think the authors wrote a series of* Funnybones *books?*

● Discuss how a blurb might be written in a tone that reflects the language patterns and genre of the book itself. You might like to look at the blurbs on one or two other familiar books to demonstrate this.

● Finally, ask the children to independently think about the main events of the story. Then let the children write a sentence or two after each of the sentence starters on the sheet to create a blurb. Encourage them to incorporate phrases or dialogue from the text.

Funnybones blurb

● Create a blurb for the back cover of *Funnybones* by completing the sentence starters below.

So you think you know skeletons? Skeletons are usually...

But let me tell you about these skeletons...

One night, something happens...

In the end...

You will love this book because...